# SAMURAI SCARECROW
## A Very Ninja Halloween

By Rubin Pingk

Simon & Schuster Books for Young Readers
New York   London   Toronto   Sydney   New Delhi

To Morgan, Sue, Chuck,
and Teresa

With special thanks to Carrie, Chloë, and Liz

SIMON & SCHUSTER BOOKS FOR YOUNG READERS
An imprint of Simon & Schuster Children's Publishing Division
1230 Avenue of the Americas, New York, New York 10020
Copyright © 2018 by Rubin Pingk
All rights reserved, including the right of reproduction in whole or in part in any form.
SIMON & SCHUSTER BOOKS FOR YOUNG READERS is a trademark of Simon & Schuster, Inc.
For information about special discounts for bulk purchases, please contact Simon & Schuster Special Sales
at 1-866-506-1949 or business@simonandschuster.com.
The Simon & Schuster Speakers Bureau can bring authors to your live event. For more information or to book an event,
contact the Simon & Schuster Speakers Bureau at 1-866-248-3049 or visit our website at www.simonspeakers.com.
Book design by Chloë Foglia and Rubin Pingk
The text for this book was set in Prova. · The illustrations for this book were rendered digitally.
Manufactured in China
0518 SCP · First Edition
10 9 8 7 6 5 4 3 2 1
Library of Congress Cataloging-in-Publication Data
Names: Pingk, Rubin, author, illustrator.
Title: Samurai Scarecrow : a very Ninja Halloween / Rubin Pingk.
Description: First edition. | New York : Simon & Schuster Books for Young Readers, (2018) | Summary: Yukio gets tired of his little sister, Kashi, questioning and copying
him, but on Halloween, when Samurai Scarecrow frightens him and demands candy, Yukio refuses to give up Kashi's.
Identifiers: LCCN 2017034121| ISBN 9781481430593 (hardcover) | ISBN 9781481430607 (ebook)
Subjects: | CYAC: Brothers and sisters—Fiction. | Halloween—Fiction. | Fear—Fiction. | Ninja—Fiction.
Classification: LCC PZ7.1.P56 Sap 2018 | DDC (E)—dc23 LC record available at https://lccn.loc.gov/2017034121

"What was that old scarecrow rhyme?" Kashi asked her brother.

At night, when the moon is full . . . SAMURAI SCARECROW wakes to sing a CREEPY lullaby:

"SHOW ME THE BIRDS NO LONGER AFRAID,

THE FEATHERED FOOLS WHO WON'T FLEE.

## "But let's run before it
# WAKES UP!"

Kashi wanted to be a **NINJA** too.
She couldn't wait to start Ninjagarten.

She asked **A LOT** of questions,
and Yukio needed a break.

Everywhere
Yukio went . . .

When Yukio carved
a pumpkin . . .

# KASHI
## FOLLOWED.

# KASHI
carved a **SIMILAR** one.

When Yukio mapped
his Halloween route . . .

It was starting
to get on Yukio's

KASHI
mapped the SAME route.

NERVES.

At night, Yukio's friends came over dressed for HALLOWEEN.

Kashi was **EXCITED** to show Yukio **HER** costume. . . .

Yukio's friends
**LAUGHED**
at the matching costumes.

Yukio's feathers were RUFFLED.

He was TIRED of Kashi copying him.

"Let's go trick-or-treating, Yuki!"

He couldn't take it ANYMORE.....

Yukio tried
to apologize . . .

but for the
FIRST
time,

Kashi
DIDN'T want
to be with him.

Into the night
went Yukio
and his friends.

Ninjas trick-or-treated all across the land. From Ninja Village . . . to the Farm District . . .

past the
Whispering Woods . . .
to where they filled their buckets
in Big Town.

With buckets full,
    Ninjas headed for home.

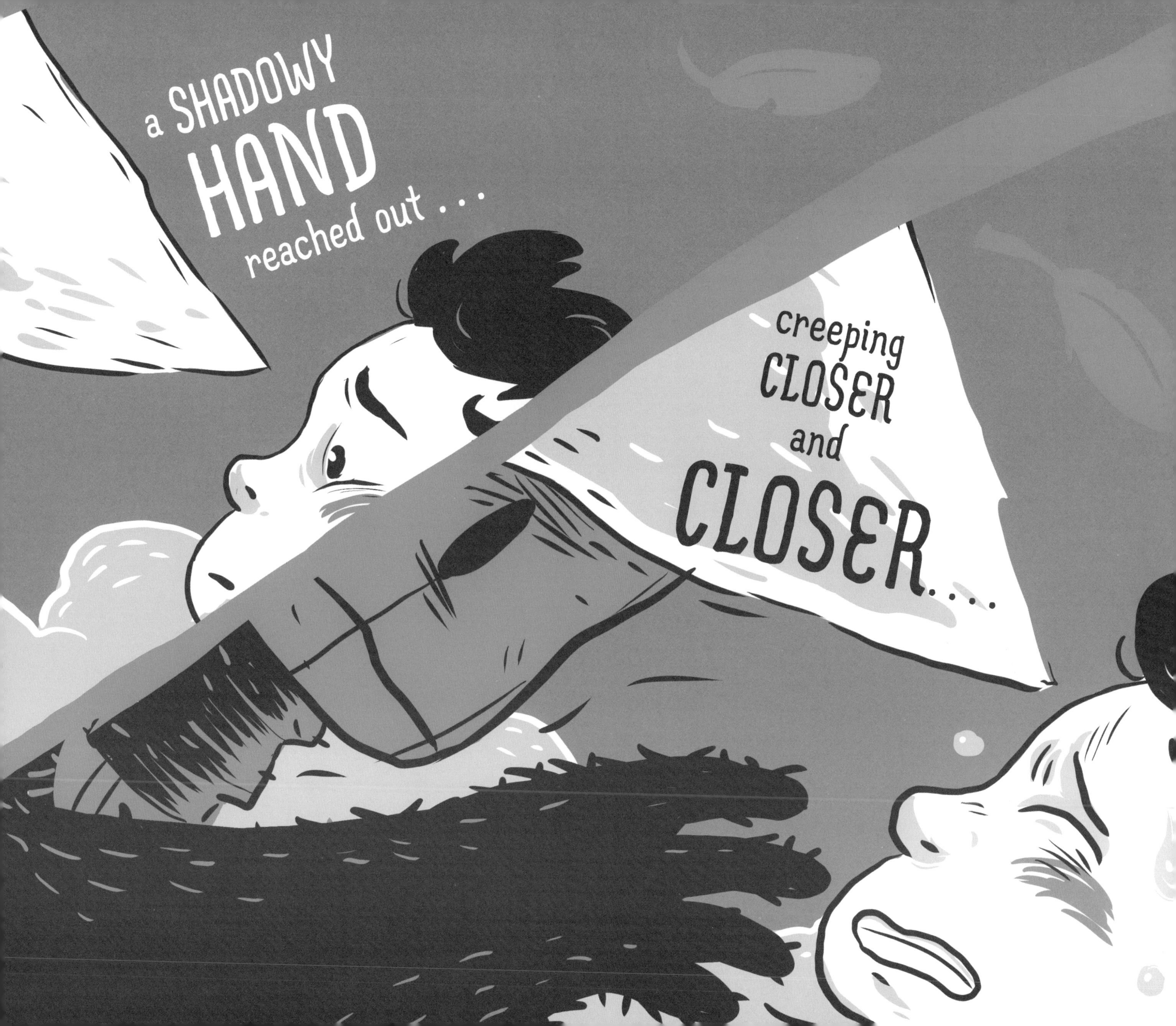
a SHADOWY
HAND
reached out . . .
creeping
CLOSER
and
CLOSER. . . .

BOOP!

Yukio wanted to be a SCARECROW too.
He couldn't wait for next Halloween.

He asked **A LOT** of questions, but Kashi didn't mind.